D0566264

PUGDOG

Andrea U'Ren

Farrar, Straus and Giroux   New York

To Mom, Dad, and Wes for their belief and investment.
And to Baby Boy, who was with me all the way through.

Copyright © 2001 by Andrea U'Ren
All rights reserved
Distributed in Canada by Douglas & McIntyre Ltd.
Color separations by Hong Kong Scanner Arts
Printed and bound in the United States of America by Worzalla
Designed by Rebecca A. Smith
First edition, 2001
1 3 5 7 9 10 8 6 4 2

Library of Congress Cataloging-in-Publication Data
U'Ren, Andrea.
    Pugdog / Andrea U'Ren.— 1st ed.
        p.   cm.
    Summary: When Mike discovers that his rough-and-tumble new puppy is a female,
he tries to make her into a dainty dog.
    ISBN 0-374-36145-5
    [1. Dogs—Fiction. 2. Sex role—Fiction.] I. Title.

PZ7.U66 Pu 2000
[E]—dc21
                                                                    00-41078

Mike didn't know much about dogs when he got his puppy.
He named it Pugdog, just because. Pugdog grew quickly.

Every day, they went to the park. Pugdog chased squirrels, rolled in the dirt, and dug big holes. Together, Mike and Pugdog played tug-of-war and fetch.

Every night after dinner, Mike gave Pugdog a fresh knucklebone to gnaw on. Then he would scratch Pugdog's big, round belly. "Good boy," he'd whisper. "Good dog."

Pugdog couldn't have been happier.

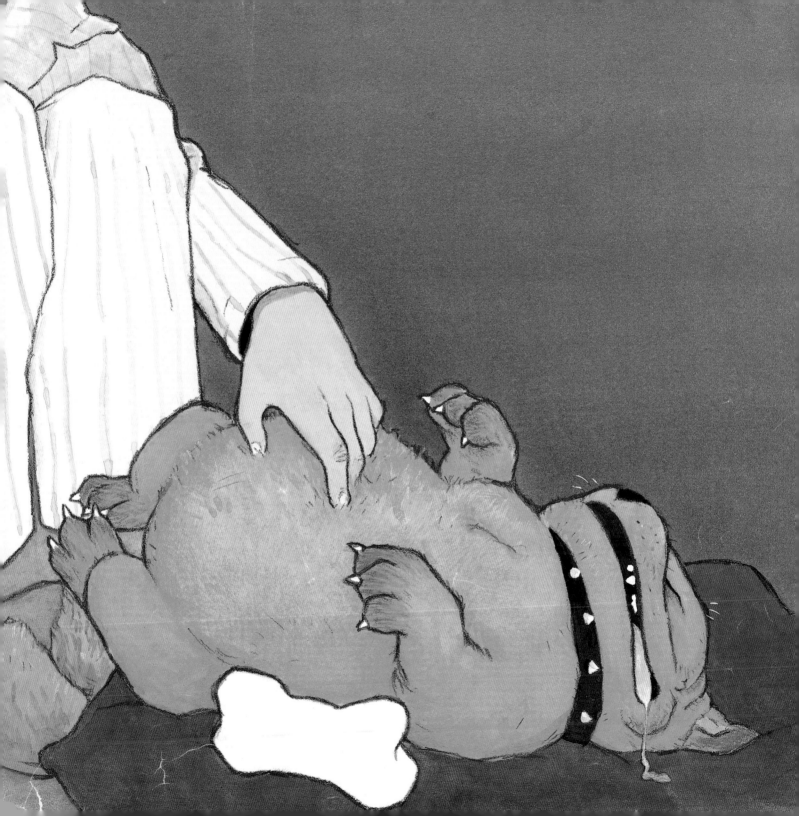

One day at the park, Pugdog injured a paw.
Mike rushed his friend to the veterinarian.
Pugdog didn't whimper once as the vet removed
a long splinter with a pair of tweezers.

"He's such a good boy!" said Mike proudly.

"*He?*" asked the vet. "*She!* Pugdog's a she! See?"

"Doggone!" Mike exclaimed. "Pugdog's a girl?
I've been treating her like a boy since day one!
She must be miserable!"

That evening, Pugdog rolled onto her back and exposed her big belly.

Mike sighed. "No, Pugdog. That's not ladylike behavior. And no more knucklebones—you need to watch your figure. You have a lot to learn, and your lessons might as well start right now."

The next morning, Pugdog had another disappointment.

Mike took her to a doggie salon. The stylist got straight to work. She gave Pugdog a bubble bath, painted her claws, and put cream on her wrinkles. Then she sprayed her with perfume and plucked out stray whiskers.

"Now for the REAL treat!" the stylist exclaimed.

"A knucklebone!" cheered Pugdog inside her head.

"An outfit! Let's put it on! You'll look pretty!"
But it made Pugdog feel silly, and was binding
her in all the wrong places, besides.

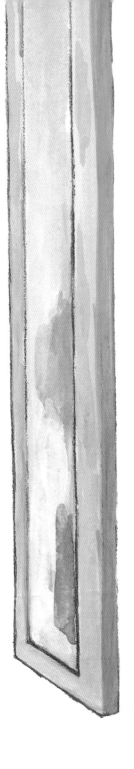

At the park, Pugdog learned that ladies didn't chase animals, not even small ones. They didn't dig holes, or roll on the ground. Fetching sticks and tug-of-war were positively out of the question.

So Mike and Pugdog went for a brisk walk (which wasn't much fun).

After much walking, they sat down to rest. Suddenly Mike gasped.

"Pugdog! Over there! Look!"

Over there was a poodle, its white head held high.

"What a dog!" Mike cried out. "She's so ladylike—she's perfect! Pugdog, that dog's something else!"

Days passed.

To make Mike happy, Pugdog tried acting like that poodle they'd seen. "Like a real lady," as Mike would say. She did her best . . .

. . . but she knew she could never compare.

   One morning, when Mike called, "Time for our walk!" Pugdog just sighed. She didn't lift her head. She didn't wag her tail, not even a twitch. "C'mon, girl," Mike said. But Pugdog was too sad. She preferred to stay in bed and remember the past.

Pugdog was no better the next day.

"Uh-oh," Mike said. "My little girl's sick!"

In no time, Pugdog was being rushed to the vet's office. But when Pugdog realized where they were going, she leapt from Mike's arms. The vet's office was where all her troubles had started!

Pugdog ran all the way to the park without once looking back.

At the park, Pugdog did what Pugdog liked
best. She chased a fat squirrel, rolled in the mud,
and dug holes of all sizes. Then she fought with
a cat, played fetch with strangers, and barked
as loudly as she pleased whenever she wanted.
At the end of the day . . .

. . . she ran straight into Mike. It was a very happy reunion.

"Pugdog!" he cried. "I thought I'd lost you for good!"

His friend was a big, slobbering mess. But Mike could see that she was happier than she'd been in ages.

"No more dainty outfits or fancy salons for you," Mike promised. "You're my Pugdog. You're perfect as you are."

Just then that poodle trotted over.

"A new pal for my Harry," the poodle's owner said. "He's such a sweetie. Always ready to make friends."

Mike groaned. "*He?* She's a *he*? Oh, Pugdog, I can see I'm the one who has a lot to learn! Can you ever forgive me?"

Pugdog barked a happy, laughing "YEP!"

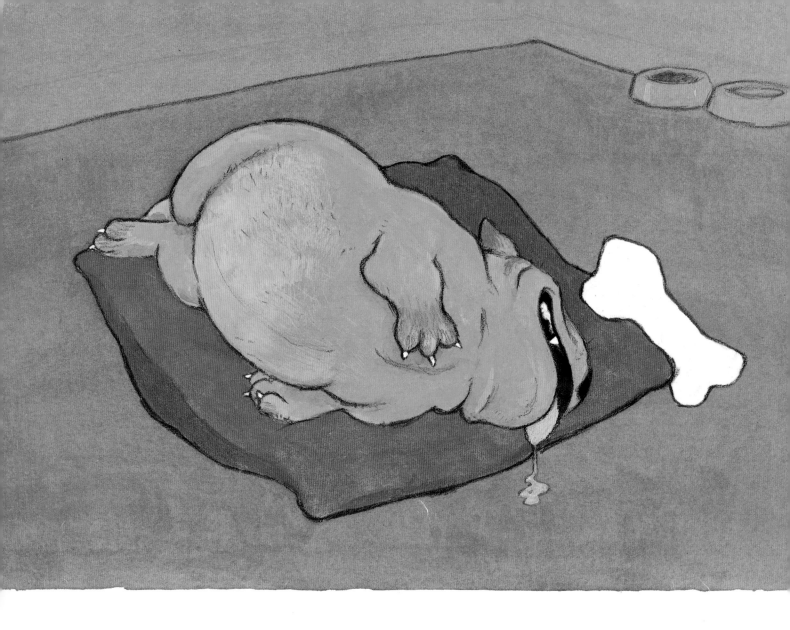

That night, Mike gave Pugdog an extra-big knucklebone and an
extra-deep belly scratch that lasted until she fell sound asleep.
From then on, Mike and Pugdog really did live happily ever after.